GIRAFFE IS LEFT OUT

A book about feeling BULLIED

SUE GRAVES
TREVOR DUNTON

GiRAFFE is LEFT OUT

Written by Sue Graves

Illustrated by Trevor Dunton

W
FRANKLIN WATTS
LONDON • SYDNEY

It was Monday morning and it was Leopard's first day at Jungle School. Miss Bird said he could sit with Monkey, Little Lion and Giraffe. She said Monkey, Little Lion and Giraffe could be Leopard's friends and help him to **feel welcome**.

But Giraffe was cross. Monkey and Little Lion were **his** friends. He **did not want** to be friends with Leopard. He **did not want** to make Leopard feel welcome.

At playtime, Monkey, Little Lion and Giraffe played football. Monkey said Leopard could play, too. But Giraffe got cross. He said Leopard **could not play**. He told Leopard to **go away**. Leopard was sad. He did not like being left out. Little Lion said Giraffe was being **very unkind**.

On Tuesday, Leopard came to school early.
He was very excited. He said it was his
birthday on Saturday. He said **everyone**
could come to his party.

Leopard gave out lots of invitations.

But he did not give an invitation to Giraffe.

Giraffe was upset. He did not like being **left out**.

Leopard told everyone about his party. He said it would be **good fun**. He said everyone would get party hats. He said there would be lots of games to play. He said there would be cakes, buns and jellies to eat. He said there would be races, too.

Giraffe felt sad. He wished he could go to Leopard's party. But Monkey said that Giraffe had been **unkind** to Leopard. Little Lion said if he **had been kinder** he might not have been left out.

That afternoon, Miss Bird said they had to work with a partner to make model boats. She said everyone had to test the boats at the end to make sure they floated. She said Giraffe and Leopard had to **work together**. But Giraffe was cross. He told Miss Bird he did not want to work with Leopard. He said Leopard was **not his friend**. But Miss Bird did not listen.

Giraffe had to cut out the boat shapes. But it was hard to do. Leopard helped him. He cut out the boat shapes really carefully. **Giraffe was pleased.**

Leopard had to stick the boat shapes together.
But it was hard to do. Giraffe helped him.
He stuck the boat shapes together really
carefully. **Leopard was pleased**.

Then they had to test the boat to see if it floated. It was very hard to do. But they helped each other. Giraffe and Leopard were pleased when the boat floated. Miss Bird said they had **worked well together**.

At playtime, Giraffe asked Leopard if he would like to play football with him, Monkey and Little Lion. They all played together.

Giraffe said Leopard was a **good player**.
Giraffe said he was sorry for being unkind.
He said he **wanted to be friends**.

The next day, Leopard had a surprise for Giraffe. He gave him a big envelope. Inside the envelope was an invitation to Leopard's birthday party. Giraffe was **very excited**. He was glad that Leopard had not left him out.

Soon it was Saturday and everyone went to Leopard's party. There were lots of party hats. There were big hats and small hats. There were tall hats and floppy hats. Giraffe thought his hat was the **best hat** of all.

21

There were lots of games to play. First they played Musical Chairs and Monkey won. He was very pleased.

Then they played Sleeping Lions and Little Lion won. He was very pleased.

Next they played
Pass the Parcel
and **Giraffe won**.
He was very,
very pleased.

Soon it was time to eat. Leopard's mum had made lots of cakes, buns and wobbly jellies. There were blue cakes and red cakes. There were sticky buns and cherry buns. There were green jellies and yellow jellies. Everyone ate it all up. It was **delicious**!

Then Leopard's dad said it was time to start the races. There was a running race and a hopping race. There was a sack race and a really silly race. Giraffe, Monkey, Little Lion and Leopard liked the **really silly** race best of all!

At last, it was time to go home. Everyone thanked Leopard for a lovely party. "Let's play together tomorrow," said Leopard. "Playing together is fun." "Yes," said Giraffe, "but let's **all** play together tomorrow. Then **no one** will be **left out** at all!"

A note about sharing this book

The *Behaviour Matters* series has been developed to provide a starting point for further discussion on children's behaviour both in relation to themselves and others. The series is set in the jungle with animal characters reflecting typical behaviour traits often seen in young children.

Giraffe is Left Out
This story explores the effect of bullying on others and the isolation felt by those who are deliberately left out of activities and games.

The book aims to encourage the children not only to examine their own behaviour towards others but also how they can get help if they are ever bullied themselves.

How to use the book
The book is designed for adults to share with either an individual child, or a group of children, and as a starting point for discussion.

The book also provides visual support and repeated words and phrases to build reading confidence.

Before reading the story
Choose a time to read when you and the children are relaxed and have time to share the story.

Spend time looking at the illustrations and talk about what the book might be about before reading it together.

Encourage children to employ a phonics first approach to tackling new words by sounding the words out.

After reading, talk about the book with the children:

- Talk about the story with the children. What was it about? Why do they think Giraffe wanted to exclude Leopard in the first place? How do they think Leopard felt about Giraffe's behaviour towards him?

- Invite the children to talk about their own experiences of being left out of things. How did they feel? What did they do about it?

- Discuss how the children react to newcomers at school. Are they always welcoming? Do they always include them in their games?

- Now ask the children if they have been new to a school. How did they feel on their first day? Do they remember someone who was particularly kind to them? How did that person behave towards them?

- Talk about the way Giraffe learnt his lesson in the story. How did he feel when he realised that he had not been invited to Leopard's party? Do the children think this was a good way to teach Giraffe a lesson?

- Extend this by discussing how the children can get help if they are bullied. Talk about the people they know and trust who can help them, for example, parents, teachers and friends. Remind them that they should never put up with being bullied and that bullying is unacceptable.

- Encourage the children in groups to co-operate on an activity, for example making a model. Encourage them to share resources and to ensure that each member of the group is allowed to contribute fully.

Franklin Watts
This edition published in Great Britain in 2016 by The Watts Publishing Group

Series Editor: Jackie Hamley
Series Designer: Cathryn Gilbert

A CIP catalogue record for this book is available
from the British Library.

ISBN 978 1 4451 4719 2 (pbk)
ISBN 978 1 4451 2773 6 (library ebook)

Printed in China

Franklin Watts
An imprint of
Hachette Children's Group
Part of The Watts Publishing Group
Carmelite House
50 Victoria Embankment
London EC4Y 0DZ

An Hachette UK Company
www.hachette.co.uk

www.franklinwatts.co.uk